PUFFIN BOOKS

NUMBER GAMES

If a hare weighs 10 lb plus half of its weight again, how much does it weigh?

If your answer to that question was 15, then you're in for a surprise! *Number Games* is jam-packed full of amazing mathematical puzzles and tricks that will test your powers of logic and keep you occupied for hours. Surprise yourself with crazy number tricks. Learn to juggle with numbers and sums, and impress your friends. Test your ingenuity on a whole host of story problems, drawing games and board games. All you need are a pocket calculator, pencil and paper, and some counters, buttons and dice – and you're ready for action!

Jutta Kirsch-Korn and Dietrich Kirsch are a married couple. They live in Waldburg, near Lake Constance in Southern Germany. They have been writing books for children for more than twenty years and many of these are published in foreign countries.

D1263459

Kirsch & Korn

NUMBER GAMES

Sixty-five puzzles to set you thinking

Translated from the German by Aran John

PUFFIN BOOKS

Contents

Puffin Books, Penguin Books Ltd, Harmondsworth, Middlesex, England
Viking Penguin Inc., 40 West 23rd Street, New York, New York 10010, U.S.A.
Penguin Books Australia Ltd, Ringwood, Victoria, Australia
Penguin Books Canada Limited, 2801 John Street, Markham, Ontario, Canada L3R 1B4
Penguin Books (N.Z.) Ltd, 182–190 Wairau Road, Auckland 10, New Zealand

First published in Germany as *Zahlen Spielerei* by
Otto Maier Verlag Ravensburg 1983
Published in Great Britain as *Number Games* in Puffin Books 1986

Copyright © Otto Maier Verlag Ravensburg, 1983
English text copyright © Penguin Books, 1986
All rights reserved

Made and printed in Great Britain by
Cox & Wyman Ltd, Reading
Filmset in Linotron Times by
Rowland Phototypesetting Ltd, Bury St Edmunds

1

Crazy numbers

Here are some number games to entertain and sometimes surprise you. You'll often find that thinking about the questions is just as important as doing some sums. Pencil and paper will help you to work out the puzzles more quickly and if you've got a pocket calculator as well then you can experiment with all sorts of different answers to the puzzles.

First things first

To start off the number games on the right left foot here are some easy puzzles to shake up your tired brain cells!

(a) How can you make the number 666 half as big again without adding anything to it?

(b) How can you show that half of 18 is 10?

(c) How can 4 and 6 together possibly make 9?

(d) How can you subtract 22 from 20 and still have 88 left?

(e) 45 from 45 can equal 45. How?

(f) How can you write the number 100 using 4 identical figures?

(g) Two positive whole numbers multiplied together make 97. Which numbers are they?

2 A hundred and one dalmatians?

A dog-breeder at a show trained his dogs to run across the stage in formation so that spectators first saw 2 dogs followed by 2 dogs, then 2 dogs between 2 dogs, then 2 dogs running after 2 dogs.

There weren't more than 6 dogs in all – so how many were there?

3 Winning the football pools!

Tom's big brother Max won a prize on the football pools. The prize was eleven thousand, eleven hundred and eleven pounds. Just imagine what that amount would look like written on the cheque!

4 How much does this hare weigh?

A hare weighs 10 lb plus half of its weight again. So what is the total weight of the hare?

5 Susan's piggy bank

Every day Susan saves some money in her piggy bank. The number of pence she puts in is half her age. She's already saved a total of 144p, and the number of days that she's been saving is exactly double her age. How old do you think Susan is?

6 Dice are like that!

Balance 6 dice one on top of the other so that the top die shows 2 spots on top. (You won't be able to see its opposite side.) In the whole stack of dice what is the total number of spots that you're unable to see?

7 Crossing out 6 numbers

This puzzle is about the numbers 111, 777 and 999.
The idea is to cross out 6 figures so that the remaining
numbers add up to 20. Which numbers would you cross
out?

8 No nutcracking!

How could you share 3 nuts between 2 friends,
so that one friend isn't given more than the other one?
The nuts must stay whole.

9 Skating figures?

On the next four pages you can give your brain a rest and exercise your pocket calculator instead! These extraordinary rows of numbers are only here to show that numbers can surprise you just as much as the sight of an elephant on roller-skates!

Take, for instance, the number 12345679. If you multiply that number by 9, or by a multiple of 9, all the answers are made up of the same repeated digit:

$$9 \times 12345679 = 111111111$$
$$2 \times 9 \times \text{ „ } = 222222222$$
$$3 \times 9 \times \text{ „ } = 333333333$$
$$4 \times 9 \times \text{ „ } = 444444444$$
$$5 \times 9 \times \text{ „ } = 555555555$$
$$6 \times 9 \times \text{ „ } = 666666666$$
$$7 \times 9 \times \text{ „ } = 777777777$$
$$8 \times 9 \times \text{ „ } = 888888888$$
$$9 \times 9 \times \text{ „ } = 999999999$$

Here's another amazing sequence of numbers:

$$1 \times 9 + 2 = 11$$
$$12 \times 9 + 3 = 111$$
$$123 \times 9 + 4 = 1111$$
$$1234 \times 9 + 5 = 11111$$
$$12345 \times 9 + 6 = 111111$$
$$123456 \times 9 + 7 = 1111111$$
$$1234567 \times 9 + 8 = 11111111$$
$$12345678 \times 9 + 9 = 111111111$$
$$123456789 \times 9 + 10 = 1111111111$$

As soon as you multiply by 8, instead of by 9, another surprising thing happens:

$$1 \times 8 + 1 = 9$$
$$12 \times 8 + 2 = 98$$
$$123 \times 8 + 3 = 987$$
$$1234 \times 8 + 4 = 9876$$
$$12345 \times 8 + 5 = 98765$$
$$123456 \times 8 + 6 = 987654$$
$$1234567 \times 8 + 7 = 9876543$$
$$12345678 \times 8 + 8 = 98765432$$
$$123456789 \times 8 + 9 = 987654321$$

10 Lucky numbers – unlucky numbers

7 is said to be a lucky number and so any number that's divisible by 7 is also meant to be lucky. And as 13 is traditionally an unlucky number, any number that's divisible by 13 is also said to bring bad luck.

So, in order to balance bad and good luck in a number, try and work out which numbers are divisible by both 7 and 13! Write down any 3-figure number; for instance, 581. Now make this a 6-figure number by writing down the same three figures after the first three, i.e. 581581. Now, it just so happens that that 6-figure number is divisible by both 7 and 13. And what's more, all numbers made up in this way will also be divisible by 11.

Can you puzzle out why this trick will always work with the numbers 7, 11 and 13?

11 Just the same old numbers?

How could you multiply the number 12345679 so that the answer would be a row of predictable and identical digits?

12 When is a nought not a nought?

Have these crazy numbers driven you mad yet? No? Well, here's a really tricky problem.

(a) How can you prove that 1 = 0?

(b) And how can you prove that 5 = 4?

(c) Everyone knows that 9 × £9 = £81
But how much is £8.99 × £8.99?

(d) What is the largest number that you can write using just 3 figures?

Let's look at the number 37. If you multiply 37 by 3, or by a multiple of 3, these are the answers you'll get:

$$3 \times 37 = 111$$
$$6 \times 37 = 222$$
$$9 \times 37 = 333$$
$$12 \times 37 = 444$$
$$15 \times 37 = 555$$
$$18 \times 37 = 666$$
$$21 \times 37 = 777$$
$$24 \times 37 = 888$$
$$27 \times 37 = 999$$

You can get another whizzy series of numbers if you multiply 91 by the numbers 1 to 9. In this you'll see that the units digit increases by 1 each time and so does the hundreds digit, whilst the tens digit decreases by 1 each time.

$$1 \times 91 = 091$$
$$2 \times 91 = 182$$
$$3 \times 91 = 273$$

$$4 \times 91 = 364$$
$$5 \times 91 = 455$$
$$6 \times 91 = 546$$
$$7 \times 91 = 637$$
$$8 \times 91 = 728$$
$$9 \times 91 = 819$$

Just look what one can do with 1s . . .

$$1 \times 1 = 1$$
$$11 \times 11 = 121$$
$$111 \times 111 = 12321$$
$$1111 \times 1111 = 1234321$$
$$11111 \times 11111 = 123454321$$
$$111111 \times 111111 = 12345654321$$
$$1111111 \times 1111111 = 1234567654321$$
$$11111111 \times 11111111 = 123456787654321$$
$$111111111 \times 111111111 = 12345678987654321$$

And how 8s can accumulate!

$$0 \times 9 + 8 = 8$$
$$9 \times 9 + 7 = 88$$
$$98 \times 9 + 6 = 888$$
$$987 \times 9 + 5 = 8888$$
$$9876 \times 9 + 4 = 88888$$
$$98765 \times 9 + 3 = 888888$$
$$987654 \times 9 + 2 = 8888888$$
$$9876543 \times 9 + 1 = 88888888$$
$$98765432 \times 9 + 0 = 888888888$$
$$987654321 \times 9 - 1 = 8888888888$$
$$9876543210 \times 9 - 2 = 88888888888$$

13 How to make 100 from 9 numbers

How could you use the numbers 1–9 to total 100?
Each number can only be used once. You can add the
numbers together and/or multiply them.

14 How to make 100 with 9 figures

Again, how can you make 100 using the numbers from
1 to 9? It's up to you to decide whether you want to use
whole numbers or fractions of numbers. Each number
from 1 to 9 can only be used once. To make 100 you must
be able just to add the numbers or fractions together.

There are at least three different answers to this
puzzle!

15 Looking for 3 numbers

Can you work out which 3 numbers, one of which is
divisible by 7, the other by 17 and the third by 27, add
up to make 100?

2

Tricks
with numbers

Now for some juggling with a few number tricks! These games are perfect to entertain your friends or your family. Some of them need pencil and paper, some need a pocket calculator, some are tricks with dice and some use magic cards.

16 Mind-reading

Ask a friend to think of a number. Then give him a couple of simple sums to do in his head and ask him to tell you the answer to those sums. You then make one simple change to the answer and, hey presto, you'll know exactly which number your friend first thought of!

(a) Ask your friend to think of any number and multiply it by 2, add 5 to the answer, then multiply that answer by 5 – and then to tell you the resulting answer.

   If you cross out the last digit of the answer and then take away 2, you'll find the number your friend first thought of.

(b) Ask your friend to think of a number and add 1 to it, double the answer, add 1 and then add the number he first thought of.

   When your friend tells you the answer, take away 3 from it and then divide the remainder by 3 and you'll get the number he first thought of!

(c) Multiply the number first thought of by 4, divide the answer by 2 and multiply the result by 7.

    To discover the number first thought of just divide the answer by 14.

(d) Double the number thought of and add any *even* number. Divide the answer by 2 and then multiply by 4. Subtract from this the added even number multiplied by 2.

    When you're told the answer to this, divide it by 4 and you'll find the number first thought of.

(e) Think of *two* numbers from 1 to 10, one of which has to be 1 bigger than the other. Multiply both numbers together and subtract the smaller number first thought of from the answer. Then multiply the resulting answer by the smaller number thought of. What is the last digit of the final answer?

    Look for this digit in the top row of this table. Then in the bottom row beneath that figure you'll find the smaller of the two numbers first thought of.

Try and puzzle out why these sums and cross-checks work and then see if you can make some tricks with numbers yourself!

17 One of 16 numbers

Your friend has chosen one out of 16 possible numbers. Here's a game to find out exactly which number it is! First, write all the 16 numbers in two columns, as shown in box A. To take an example, the 16 numbers could be 1–16. (But they could be any other numbers and in any order.) The only condition is that no number can be used more than once.

Let's say that your friend has thought of the number 5.

You ask him which column the number appears in and he'll say in the first column.

Then you write out the second column unchanged (see box B). Then you write out the numbers of the first column down both sides of the column in turn: 1 on the left, 2 on the right, 3 on the left, and so on.

Then you ask again which column the number is in. The answer will be: the first column. So the number must be 1, 3, 5 or 7.

After that, write out the middle column from B unchanged into the C box (see picture). Then copy the numbers of the first B column down both sides of the column in turn and immediately follow on with the third B column as well.

Now ask again which column the number is in. Answer: in the first column. So the number must be either 1 or 5. Now again copy down the second column unchanged and rearrange the numbers of the other two columns in order of increase – as shown in D. Now for the last time ask which column is the number in?

The answer: in the third column. Now you know that the number must be 5!

18 Looking 2 dice in the eye

Supposing you want to find out – without looking! – what score a friend has made when he's thrown 2 dice. First you ask your friend to double the spots on the first die, then add 5, multiply that sum by 5 and add the spots on the second die. Your friend then tells you the answer.

To find out the score on each die, subtract 25 from the answer your friend has given you. The tens digit of the resulting number will be the same as the spots on the first die, and the units digit will be the same as the spots on the second die.

19 Seven magic cards

You can easily make yourself some magic cards in the standard card size (approx. 6 × 9 cm). On each of the seven cards use a typewriter to copy out the following series of numbers:

I.

1 3 5 7 9 11 13 15 17 19 21 23
25 27 29 31 33 35 37 39 41 43
45 47 49 51 53 55 57 59 61 63
65 67 69 71 73 75 77 79 81 83
85 87 89 91 93 95 97 99

II.

2 3 6 7 10 11 14 15 18 19 22
23 26 27 30 31 34 35 38 39 42
43 46 47 50 51 54 55 58 59 62
63 66 67 70 71 74 75 78 79 82
83 86 87 90 91 94 95 98 99

III.

4 5 6 7 12 13 14 15 20 21 22
23 28 29 30 31 36 37 38 39 44
45 46 47 52 53 54 55 60 61 62
63 68 69 70 71 76 77 78 79 84
85 86 87 92 93 94 95 100

IV.

8 9 10 11 12 13 14 15 24 25 26
27 28 29 30 31 40 41 42 43 44
45 46 47 56 57 58 59 60 61 62
63 72 73 74 75 76 77 78 79 88
89 90 91 92 93 94 95

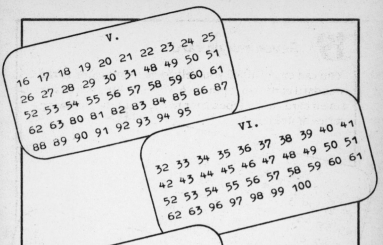

V.

16 17 18 19 20 21 22 23 24 25
26 27 28 29 30 31 48 49 50 51
52 53 54 55 56 57 58 59 60 61
62 63 80 81 82 83 84 85 86 87
88 89 90 91 92 93 94 95

VI.

32 33 34 35 36 37 38 39 40 41
42 43 44 45 46 47 48 49 50 51
52 53 54 55 56 57 58 59 60 61
62 63 96 97 98 99 100

VII.

64 65 66 67 68 69 70 71 72 73
74 75 76 77 78 79 80 81 82 83
84 85 86 87 88 89 90 91 92 93
94 95 96 97 98 99 100

Now comes the clever bit. With this trick you'll be able to 'guess' whichever number, from 1 to 100, any of your friends has thought of.

You just need to show a friend your seven cards one after the other. The friend then has to tell you where his number has appeared.

Then on each of the cards he's picked out, read out the very first number which appears in the upper left-hand corner. Add the numbers together and the answer will be the number first thought of!

20 A number code

For this trick you'll first of all need the following code for the letters:

A	B	C	D	E	F	G	H	I	J
1	2	3	4	5	6	7	8	9	10

K	L	M	N	O	P	Q	R
11	12	13	14	15	16	17	18

S	T	U	V	W	X	Y	Z
19	20	21	22	23	24	25	26

Your friend thinks of a name (e.g., Carl) and adds together in his head the numbers which correspond to the letters of the name (e.g., 3 + 1 + 18 + 12 = 34). Then for each letter of the name he takes the number corresponding to that letter away from the total (here, 34) and writes the answers on a piece of paper.

Your friend then tells you these numbers. You add the numbers together (= 102) and divide the sum by a number which is 1 smaller than the number of letters in the name (so here it's 3; and 102 ÷ 3 = 34). From this answer you subtract, in turn, the numbers written on the piece of paper (34 − 31 = 3, and so on). Then, if you look up the resulting numbers, 3, 1, 18, 12, in the code, you'll find the corresponding letters.

21   You know the rest

Your friend thinks of a 3-digit number and writes it down. Then he writes down the same digits but in the reverse order. Then he subtracts the smaller number from the bigger one but only tells you the units figure of the resulting number.

But you know the rest of the number anyway! How? Because the middle number will always be 9 and the two numbers either side of that 9 added together will always make 9 (e.g., 321 − 123 = 198).

22 When's your friend's birthday?

Just ask a friend to do one small sum in her head, and you'll soon know when her birthday is! Your friend multiplies the day number of the date of her birthday by 3, then adds 5 to the sum, multiplies the total by 4, adds the day number plus the month number and finally subtracts 20. She then tells you the answer!

Now you divide that answer by 13. The number of times that 13 will divide into it completely will be the day number, and the number left over by the division sum will be the month number.

Try it out!

What! no mental arithmetic?

But this is so much easier . . .

23 How to know the answer first!

Ask someone to think of any number, then to double it, join a 4 to the end of it, halve the total and subtract the number first thought of.

You'll always be able to say that you already know the answer: it's 2! It's true!

3

Number
stories

Now for a bit of logic plus a bit of maths – so a
notebook will be useful here and then you can easily jot
down the important facts in the right order. And step
by step you'll track down the answer.

24 Buying time

Stan Speed, a rather crafty fellow, bought himself a wristwatch for £45 and a watch strap for £5. He'd only just left the shop when he turned around and went back in and chose a clock costing £75. Stan Speed said to the jeweller, 'I've already paid you £50 and now I'll give you another £25 for this clock. So you've got £75 altogether.' Then he disappeared for good with the expensive clock, but left the watch strap behind in his hurry. At first the jeweller thought the swap was quite satisfactory, but later, when he'd thought about it a bit, he realized that he'd been swindled.

Do you know how much money he lost?

25 The apple game

Anne Appleby's favourite number game has to be played in the autumn, when fruit is falling from the trees. To play the game Anne puts a basket down on the grass and arranges 100 apples next to it in a straight line. The basket, the first apple and all the other apples must be placed one step apart. Then one player has to collect all 100 apples, taking each apple separately and

placing it in the basket. (The basket always stays in the same place.) The other players have to count the number of steps the player has taken while collecting the apples. But perhaps you can work out in advance how many steps would be taken altogether?

26 A merchant of Venice

One day in Venice a merchant accidentally dropped a 13 kg stone weight on the floor. It broke into 3 pieces. When the merchant weighed the pieces he found that, by some chance, each piece happened to weigh an exact round number of kgs. What's more, he found out that with these 3 new weights he could weigh any whole number of kgs from 1 to 13.

How much does each broken piece weigh? And how can these weights be used to weigh out 1 to 13 kgs?

27 Heartbeats

Can you guess how many times
your heart beats in an hour?
It's about 5,000 times. From
that, can you work out how
many beats the heart has made
by the time a person reaches
the age of sixty?

28 Deciphering a fishy note

The fishmonger Angus McTavish was well known for
the excellent smoked salmon he sold. He was very
proud of his smoked salmon, so he kept a note of how
much money he'd made from selling it.

Last Saturday his note managed to get wedged
between two sides of salmon. By the time the
fishmonger found it again some of the figures had got
smudged by salmon!

Can you work out what was originally written on the
note?

29 Ruby's rings

Ruby has two silver rings which she likes to wear all the time. She never puts both rings together on the same finger and never wears one on a thumb.

How many different ways can Ruby wear her rings?

30 A ball pyramid

Leo, Theo and Cleopatra like building pyramids with brightly coloured plastic balls. (How they manage to make the pyramids stay up is their secret!) In this picture they're building a 3-sided ball pyramid. There are 9 balls on each side of the bottom row.

How many balls will the finished pyramid contain?

31 | A fairly chronic family chronicle

Wherever Nina turns up she can't resist telling the puzzling saga of her family and relations. So, let's meet Nina and hear what her story is!

'My age plus my brother-in-law's age equals my father's age; my age added to my brother's adds up to my brother-in-law's age; in 2 years' time my brother will be half as old as my father; my mother's age plus my niece's age added together make the same as my father's age; in 4 years' time I'll be a third of my mother's age; my father is 50 years old!'

Then Nina always asks, 'How old is each member of my family?' And you'll probably say to her, 'Oh, do shut up and leave me alone!'

32 | 11 dice for 2 princes

Once upon a time there was a very rich king.
Every day he and his two sons used to play a game with 11 different dice made of solid gold. There were 5 dice which had sides 1 cm long, 4 dice with sides

2 cm long and the remaining 2 dice had sides 3 and 4 cm long respectively.

One day the king wanted to give the dice to his sons as a present. 'If you find out how these 11 dice could be shared equally between the two of you, so that each of you gets the same amount of gold, I'll give you the dice. And no die must be cut up – after all we'll still want to be able to play our game of dice together!'

The younger prince solved the puzzle first. Can you solve it too?

33 The donkey and the mule

A tired donkey and a hungry mule were on the way from Poggibonsi to San Giminiano. Both of them were staggering along under their loads, which consisted of several jars of olive oil. All the jars were the same size. The donkey complained to the mule about the weight of his load, but the mule replied, 'You've nothing to moan about. If one of the jars in your load was added to my load then I'd have twice as much to carry as you would. But if one jar from my load was transferred to your load then we'd have the same amount to carry.'

How many jars of olive oil is each animal carrying?

34 The bookworm and his book

Felix Cleverdick loved going to the library to look things up in the encyclopedia. So for his birthday his parents decided to give him a huge two-volume encyclopedia of his own. Each volume had exactly 500 pages. Felix was thrilled at his present and immediately opened the first volume and solemnly wrote his name on the flyleaf.

At that very moment a bookworm fell off the ceiling and landed unnoticed on the book and quietly sat on page 1. Felix snapped the book shut, but the bookworm took a deep breath to make himself small and wasn't hurt. Felix then stood the two new books neatly in order on the shelf. The worm immediately started to nibble away at the nice new book. He nibbled continuously until one day Felix opened his encyclopedia and saw the worm sitting on page 500 of the second volume.

Supposing that the bookworm eats 5 pages a day or 1 book cover per day, how long did it take the bookworm to eat from page 1 of the first volume to page 500 of the second volume?

35   Paying off debts

Peter owed Paula £1. They agreed
that Peter would pay back half
this sum, i.e., 50p, to Paula on
3 December. Then the following
day he'd again pay half of the
sum owed, i.e., 25p, and
so on – the next day half of
what he'd owed the
previous day.

    When would Peter have
repaid the £1?

36   What's special about the number 36?

Ben Snipsworth's favourite number was 36. He liked
the way that 36 was made up of 4 numbers and that if
you added 2 to one of the numbers, subtracted 2
from another number, multiplied the third
number by 2 and divided the fourth number by 2,
and then added the resulting four numbers
together, they would
still add up to 36!

    Can you divide
36 the way Ben
Snipsworth did?

37 The meeting of two strange snails

One morning a snail was sitting at the foot of a fir tree 9.6 metres high. He decided to start sliding upwards. He slid up 30 cm every day and slipped back 20 cm every night.

At the same moment another strange snail sitting at the top of the same fir tree started to slide downwards. Every day he slid down 40 cm and every night he crept back up 20 cm.

How many days will it be until the two snails meet?

38 Run, rabbit, run!

Every evening Mr Miraculo the magician and his white rabbits perform in a theatre. Last night Mr Miraculo

gave someone in the audience half of all his magic rabbits, plus half a rabbit. Then Mr Miraculo gave half of the remaining rabbits, plus half a rabbit, to another startled spectator in the audience. Then to a third person he gave half of the rabbits then left, plus half a rabbit. Finally, he gave the last rabbit to a fourth person in the theatre.

Of course, Mr Miraculo wouldn't dream of dividing a rabbit in half, or anything like that, even by magic. So what's the total number of rabbits that he's enchanted?

39 The 7 regulars

7 men were regular customers at 'Harry's Milkbar'. Herbie went there every day, Hugo every second day, Humphrey every third day, Hank every fourth day, Hubert every fifth day, Horace every sixth day and Hugh every seventh day. One morning by chance they all happened to sit down together at the Milkbar.

Harry, the owner of the Milkbar, promised to buy them a round of milkshakes the next time they all came together on the same day to his Milkbar. Of course, he really didn't think that they would meet up again for a very long time.

But exactly when would the 7 regulars next meet?

40 Will the tortoise win?

2,500 years ago in Greece, a professor called Xenon Eleates wrote this fable as evidence against the Rules of Movement:

Achilles, who was a fast runner, agreed to run a race against a tortoise, for a bet. The tortoise was given a start of one league. Achilles could run 10 times as fast as the tortoise, but even so he was never able to catch up with it. Xenon's explanation for this was that when Achilles reached the point where the tortoise had been when Achilles started off, the tortoise would have moved a bit further on, and so on ad infinitum.

Why do you think that Xenon's fable was wrong?

41 The three clocks

One midnight the Topsyturvy family were suddenly awakened when 3 of their clocks all chimed together. The noise was incredible. The Topsyturvys knew that 1 of their clocks always told the right time, 1 was always 10 minutes fast and 1 was always 10 minutes slow.

How many days would it take before the 3 clocks all struck 12 together again?

4

Drawing and board games

You can play these boredom-beating games on your own. Enjoy yourself; try them and see! You can use pencil and paper, dice, buttons, counters (or small coins with coloured stickers on them) and of course your calculator will help too.

42 Figures and numbers

How many different 4-figure numbers can you make using these 4 number blocks?

43 The total is 6

Try to write the numbers 1, 2 and 3 one beneath the other 3 times in the squares shown so that they make a square of numbers. In the square the numbers must be placed so that in each line of figures (horizontally, vertically or diagonally) the numbers always add up to 6. Is this possible?

44 The answer is 13

Place the numbers 1–8 on the dots on this diagram so that the 3 figures on each line always add up to 13.

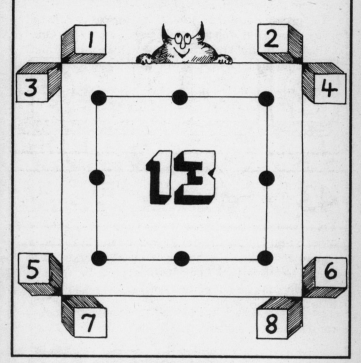

45 Three paper shapes

A rectangular piece of paper, twice as long as it's wide, can be divided into 8 equal squares using only 3 straight cutting lines.

Find some scrap paper to try this one out!

46 The three heirs

3 people inherited an unusual legacy: 15 wine casks!
Each of them was meant to inherit the same amount of
wine and the same number of wine casks.

The problem was that 5 of the 15 wine casks were full
up(F), 5 were half-full (H) and 5 were empty (E). One
of the heirs thought over the problem for a minute and
worked out the answer. Can you work it out too?

47 Brilliant! 10 buttons

Can you put 10 buttons in 5 straight lines so that there
are 4 buttons in each line? You're a real number games
star if you get the answer to this one!

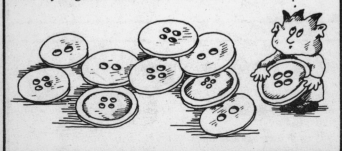

48 The penny cross

There are 9 1p pieces lying on the table in the shape of a cross. Take the top coin and bottom coin away completely and see if you can still manage to have 5 coins in each line.

49 The 8-dot chess-board

There are 8 dots to be placed on a chess-board ($8 \times 8 = 64$ squares). There must be no more than one dot in any row of squares – up or down, across or diagonal. It's your move!

50 Changing places

4 white counters and 4 blue counters are lined up in a row:

Now, in just 4 moves, re-arrange them so that all the white counters are next to each other and all the blue counters are next to each other, as shown:

For each move you can only change the positions of counters which are next to each other. The order of the rest of the line and the space between the counters mustn't be altered.

When you've managed to get all the blue counters next to each other and all the white counters next to each other, try and return the counters to their original order, using just 4 moves!

51 Ships on the channel

The Canape Channel is so narrow that only 1 ship can pass through it at a time. One day 4 ships arrived at the

channel, 2 going in each direction. They met just where the channel had a small passing-place which could only be occupied by just 1 ship at a time.

How should the ships manoeuvre so as to continue on their voyages as quickly as possible?

52 1 orchard and 4 brothers

4 brothers inherited an orchard from their uncle, Jonathan Bramley. The orchard had 12 fruit trees. The brothers agreed to share the orchard into 4 equal areas in which each of them would have the same number of fruit trees. How did they work this out? Is there more than one way?

53 Do you think you've got the right saw for it?

This peculiar piece of wood has to be sawn into 4 equal parts which must be the same shape as the original piece of wood.

54 The square rectangle

Joe Jones was a master joiner. He wanted to cut a square table-top from a rectangular piece of wood. The

piece of wood measured 40 × 90 cm but the table-top had to measure 60 × 60 cm. So Joe Jones cut the wood into two equal pieces which, if placed together, would make the required square.

How did he work this out?

55 The paper-knot

It's fairly difficult to work out mathematically, and to draw, a pentagon with 5 equal sides. But you can easily by-pass the maths bit, because it's much easier to make a pentagon out of paper.

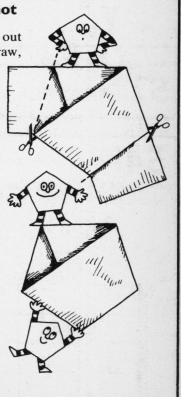

First cut a strip of paper at least 7 or 8 times as long as it's wide. Then interweave the paper as closely as possible into a flat knot (see picture), without crumpling the paper. Cut off the overhanging ends of the knot and you'll have a perfectly regular pentagon!

56 4 into 3

Can you draw a 4-sided figure which can be divided into 3 triangles by one straight line?

57 Flower-boxes

Try and re-arrange the flowers among these 36 squares in the flower-boxes so that there are 3 flowers in each horizontal and in each vertical row.

58 The cake

One tea time the Crumbs family, 4 children and
4 grown-ups, were looking forward to eating a
magnificent round cake. The youngest child, Tina,
worked out that she could cut into the cake just 3 times
and manage to divide it so that all the adults had the
same size piece and all the children had the same size
piece.

Could you cut the cake like that too?

59 Lord Bagshot's window

About 200 years ago, Lord Bagshot decided that his
library was far too gloomy; there wasn't enough light to
read his books properly!
So he decided to
rebuild one of the
library windows. The
window was originally
1 m high and 1 m wide.
When Lord Bagshot had
doubled the size of the
window it still measured
1 m high and 1 m wide.
How was that possible?

60 Mosaic squares

Here are some games about shapes. You can trace these shapes on to paper and then cut them out.

(a) Can you fit these five triangles together to make a square?

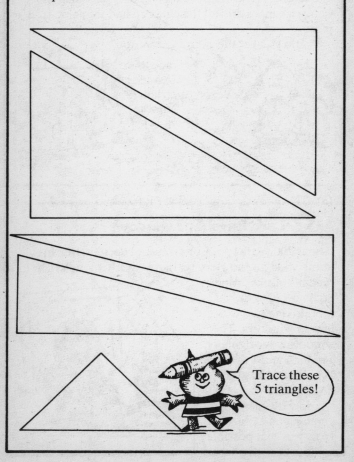

Trace these 5 triangles!

(b) Now cut out 4 right-angled triangles and a small square and try to fit the 5 shapes together to make a big square.

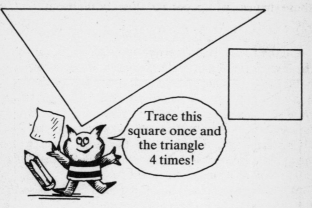

(c) This game is quite tricky! Fit together these 8 shapes into a regular square.

61 An Alpine quarrel

In a pasture in the Alps there was a quarrel brewing.
3 farmers who weren't on speaking terms had mountain
shelters A, B and C in the pasture. Shelter B was built
up against the rock face of the mountain.

On the rock face on the opposite side of the pasture
there were three mountain springs, a, b and c. Spring a
belonged to A's hut, b belonged to B's hut and c
belonged to C's hut. Farmer A had already dug a ditch
from spring a directly to his hut. Now, the other two
farmers, not to be outdone, also wanted to have water
channels going to their huts. As the farmers weren't on
speaking terms none of them wanted his channel to
cross another farmer's channel.

Where can farmers B and C dig their channels so that
they can avoid having yet another quarrel?

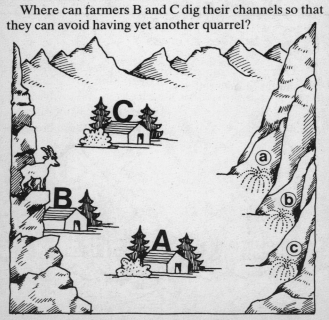

62 The quickest route

Paco has forgotten to refill his rabbit's water bowl.
So can you work out what is the quickest route for Paco
to take from his house to the stream and then from the
stream to the hutch with the water?

● HOUSE

RABBIT-HUTCH
●

~~~~~~~~~~~~~~~~~~
STREAM

63 8 bridges to cross

The old town of Bridgeville in West Carolina, USA, is
built on 2 beautiful islands in the middle of the Dream
River. 8 bridges have been built to link the town's 2
islands and the mainland. Is it possible to work out a
route by which you could cycle across all these bridges –
but only across each bridge once?

64 A question of conservation

In the small village of Nettlesop there is a square duckpond. The villagers plan to double the size of the pond, but want to keep it shaped as a square. However, 2 fine trees stand at each corner of the duckpond and the villagers wouldn't dream of cutting them down or flooding them in water.

So how do the villagers solve the problem of enlarging the duckpond while still saving the trees?

65 An easy puzzle to end with

How can you draw a triangle with a single straight line?

Answers

1(a) If you write 666 upside down, then it's 999.

1(b) If you draw a straight line halfway down across the number 18 you'll get two 10s.

1(c) If you reverse the Roman numeral for 6, VI, and turn it upside down and write it under IV, the Roman numeral for 4, then it will look like IX, which is the Roman numeral for 9.

1(d) $\quad$ X X
$\quad$ − 2 2
$\quad$ = 8 8
XX is the Roman numeral for 20, but it's also two Roman 10s written side by side.

1(e) $\quad$ 9 8 7 6 5 4 3 2 1 (which add up to 45)
$\quad$ − 1 2 3 4 5 6 7 8 9 (which add up to 45)
$\quad$ = 8 6 4 1 9 7 5 3 2 (which add up to 45)

1(f) 99% (= 100).

1(g) 1 and 97.

2 4 dogs.

3 12, 111.

4 20 lb (not 15 lb as you might expect).

5 She's 12 years old.

6 The spots on opposite sides of a die always add up to 7. So the spots hidden in this pile must add up to 40.

7 $\quad$ ■ 1 1
$\quad$ ■ ■ ■
$\quad$ + ■ ■ 9
$\quad$ = $\quad$ 2 0

8 You give 1 nut to one friend and 2 nuts to the other friend. Then *one* doesn't get more than the other!

10 If the numbers are divisible by 7, 11 *and* 13, they must at least be the product of these numbers ($7 \times 11 \times 13 = 1,001$) or a multiple of it. The number 1,001 is of course perfect for this trick with any three-figure number, as the thousands digit and the units digit are the same – so the 6-figure number will always be divisible by 7, 11 and/or 13!

11 See puzzle number 9!

12(a) As $1 \times 0 = 0$
and $0 \times 0 = 0$
then $1 \times 0 = 0 \times 0$
If you divide both sides by 0 then $1 = 0$.

What's the trick there? In the last sum: both sides of an equation were indeed divided by the same factor, but division by 0 is meaningless!

12(b) The first equation is:
$3 + 4 = 7$
Then you add the magic equation:
$4 \times 3 + 4 \times 4 - 5 \times 7 = 4 \times 3 + 4 \times 4 - 5 \times 7$
that makes:
$5 \times 3 + 5 \times 4 - 5 \times 7 = 4 \times 3 + 4 \times 4 - 4 \times 7$
or: $5 (3 + 4 - 7) = 4 (3 + 4 - 7)$
Then divide the equation by $(3 + 4 - 7)$ and the result is: $5 = 4$

Where's the mistake here? In the line before last both sides of the equation were indeed divided by the same factor, but division by 0 $(3 + 4 - 7 = 0)$ is meaningless!

12(c) The problem is unsolvable, because you can't multiply a *concrete* number (e.g., £12, 8 kg . . .) by another concrete number, so you *can't* multiply £8.99 by £8.99.

12(d) You might think the number is 999 but actually it's 9^{9^9}. That's how one writes powers. 9^9 really means that 9 must be multiplied by itself 9 times. $9^9 = 387,420,489$. Now the other 9 (the third from the right) must be multiplied by itself that many times. The resulting number is so huge that it would be very difficult even to write it down: it has 369,693,100 figures.

Supposing that one writes 4 figures per centimetre, then the number would be 924.23275 km long!

13 $9 \times 8 + 7 + 6 + 5 + 4 + 3 + 2 + 1 = 100$.

14

$74\frac{9}{18}$	or	97	or	98
$+ 25\frac{3}{6}$		$+ 1$		$+ \frac{3}{6}$
$= 100$		$+ \frac{2}{3}$		$+ \frac{27}{54}$
		$+ \frac{4}{8}$		$+ 1$
		$+ \frac{5}{6}$		$= 100$
		$= 100$		

15 7, 17 and 27 added together make 51. If you subtract 51 from 100 you're left with 49, which is 7×7.
As $1 \times 7 + 7 \times 7 = 56$, the answer is: $56 + 17 + 27 = 100$.

24 The first purchase was completely correct. Stan Speed then returned to the shop with the watch (worth £45) and by mistake left behind the watch strap (worth £5). So he tricked the jeweller out of the remaining £45.

25 10,100 steps.
Added together there would be: 2, 4, 6, 8 . . ., up to 200 steps. Instead of working out a long series of numbers, there is a quick way. Write the series of numbers again, but this time in the reverse order – 200, 198 . . . 4, 2 – then add them to the first series of numbers and there will be 100 terms all of 202, giving 20,200. But, as this is twice the sum we want, it must be divided by 2.

26 1, 3 and 9 kg.

1 kg = 1 kg	8 kg = 9 − 1 kg
2 kg = 3 − 1 kg	9 kg = 9 kg
3 kg = 3 kg	10 kg = 9 + 1 kg
4 kg = 3 + 1 kg	11 kg = (9 + 3) − 1 kg
5 kg = 9 − (3 + 1) kg	12 kg = 9 + 3 kg
6 kg = 9 − 3 kg	13 kg = 9 + 3 + 1 kg
7 kg = (9 + 1) − 3 kg	

27 2,629,800,000 heartbeats (a year is calculated as 365¼ days).

28 36 kgs at £12.46 per kg = £448.56.

29 56 different ways.

30 165 balls. Add up the number of balls in the pyramid layer by layer, starting at the bottom and working up to the very top ball ($45 + 36 + 28 + 21 + 15 + 10 + 6 + 3 + 1$).

31 Nina is 13 years old, her brother-in-law is 37, her father is 50, her brother is 24, her mother is 47 and her niece is 3.

32   One prince was given the largest die, the other prince got the remaining 10 dice.

   The puzzle really hinges on the cubic volume of the dice which determines how much gold they contained: $5 \times 1 \text{ cm}^3 = 5 \text{ cm}^3$, $4 \times 8 \text{ cm}^3 = 32 \text{ cm}^3$ and $1 \times 27 \text{ cm}^3 = 27 \text{ cm}^3$. So these three dice together have the same amount of gold in them as the die with a volume of $1 \times 64 \text{ cm}^3 = 64 \text{ cm}^3$.

33   The donkey has 5 jars and the mule has 7. If it seems difficult to work out the answer, try using two equations:
$$M - 1 = D + 1$$
$$2(D - 1) = M + 1.$$
Then do you know how to resolve those equations?

34   Felix put the two volumes back 'in order' on the shelf, so volume 1 was on the left and volume 2 on the right. So page 1 of volume 1 and page 500 of volume 2 were only separated by 2 bookcovers. So the worm only needed 2 days to eat that distance!

35   Never! Even when Peter's debt got down to the smallest coin possible, a 1p, he'd still owe half that sum, and so on for ever.

36 $6 + 2 = 8$
   $10 - 2 = 8$
   $4 \times 2 = 8$
   $16 \div 2 = 8$
   $6 + 10 + 4 + 16 = 36$

37   They'll meet on the 31st day of their travels and not, as you might have expected, on the 32nd day, because each day the snails move towards each other and on the *morning* of the 31st day they are 60 cm away from each other. During that *day* the first snail slides up 30 cm and the second snail slides down 40 cm. So they'd creep past each other then.

38   15 rabbits.

39   In 420 days' time. (420 is the 'lowest common denominator', i.e., the smallest number which is exactly divisible by 1, 2, 3, 4, 5, 6 and 7.)

40 This devious wrong conclusion completely omits the important *time* factor. Supposing that Achilles runs one league in one hour, then the tortoise will in the meantime travel 1/10 league. Achilles runs 1/10 league in 1/10 hour. The periods of time thus decrease for Achilles by 1/10, so 1 + 1/10 + 1/100 + 1/1000 . . . hours = 1.111 . . . hours. Although this decimal point is endlessly recurring, the time actually has a definite, finite value (i.e., 1⅑). After the course of this time Achilles catches up with the tortoise and begins to overtake it. In terms of leagues you could say that while the tortoise has covered ⅑ of the next league, Achilles has advanced by 10/9, i.e., 1⅑ leagues. Thus both Achilles and the tortoise have reached the same place at the same point of time.

41 It would be 72 days before the fast clock struck 12 at the same time as the correct clock, and it would be 60 days before the slow clock chimed with the correct clock. So all 3 of them would strike together in 360 (5 × 72 or 6 × 60) days' time.

42 Twelve:

9910	9091	1099
9901	9019	0991
9190	1990	0919
9109	1909	0199

43

1	3	2
3	2	1
2	1	3

44

8	3	2
4		6
1	7	5

45 First cut: divide the rectangle into 2 equal halves.
Second cut: put the 2 pieces one on top of each other and cut both in half (so making 4 equal rectangles).
Third cut: again put all the pieces on top of each other and cut them in half (making 8 equal squares).

46

F	F	F	F	F
H	H	H	H	H
E	E	E	E	E

47

48 You also take the coins from the extreme right and left of the cross and place them on the coin in the middle so that 3 coins will be one on top of the other.

49 Here's why there isn't a simple answer to this one! There are 40,320 possible ways of placing 8 dots on 64 squares – but there are only 92 different solutions to the puzzle set in this question! Here is one of them:

The chess-board can then be turned around by 90°, 3 times, making 4 different arrangements of the dots. Then these 4 possible arrangements can also be reversed, i.e., as seen in a mirror. However, in spite of these 8 possible arrangements, they are all variations of just one solution – and there are 92 solutions in all!

50 Number the positions of the counters from left to right 1–8 and write 9 and 10 under the next two empty places along the line.

1   2   3   4   5   6   7   8   9   10,

Then these are the moves: 2 and 3 to 9 and 10
                          5 and 6 to 2 and 3
                          8 and 9 to 5 and 6
                          1 and 2 to 8 and 9

Then, to return the coins to exactly where they were at the start in only 4 moves, just repeat the moves described above, but in reverse order.

51 Try working it out using numbered counters:
Ship no. 3 goes into the passing-place
Ships nos. 2 and 1 sail straight on
Ship no. 3 can now sail out of the passing-place and continue on its way
Ships nos. 1 and 2 go back past the passing-place
Ship no. 4 sails into the passing-place
Ships nos. 1 and 2 can now go past the passing-place and sail on
Then ship no. 4 can sail out of the passing-place and sail on.

52 There are two ways to work this out:

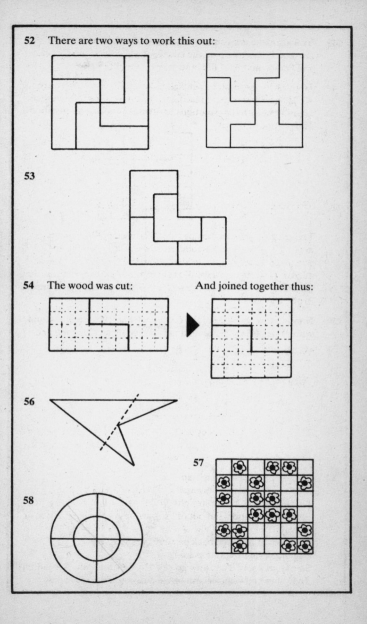

53

54 The wood was cut: And joined together thus:

56

57

58

59 The original window was like this:

Later it looked like this:

60(a)

60(b)

60(c)

61

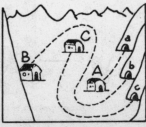

62 This is the shortest route:

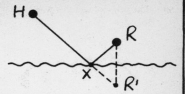

First of all you find point R^1, which is the same distance from the stream as R is on the other side. The line joining R and R^1 must cross the line of the stream vertically. Now join H and R^1. Draw a line from the point X – where the line HR^1 crosses the stream – to R. Now, the lines HX and then XR are the shortest distance between H and R.

(If you make a larger drawing then you can test other possible answers.)

63 Yes it is possible! If you started on one island and finished on the other island. E.g.:

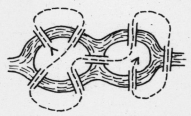

64 The dotted lines show how the duckpond was enlarged:

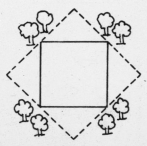

65 You draw a line across a corner and the two lines already there make the other two sides of the triangle!